The

Brotherhood

Don Allen

Cover, Shutterstock stock photo (1025635576)

ISBN: 979-8-9880521-1-1

eISBN: 979-8-9880521-0-4

Publisher: Don Allen

Also by Don Allen

<u>Sean Murphy Series</u>
Satisfaction
Chaos
The Launderer

<u>Other</u>
Dog Walker
Check for Junk

Dedication:

To My three granddaughters

who add a spark to my life

1 In the Beginning

It was my first day back in the office after being shot in the shoulder by a drug kingpin's nephew. Heading to the break room, I was receiving high-fives. I had been recuperating for several months, perhaps a month or two more than necessary, but hey, I deserved it. I visited my daughter Wanda and the twins in their new home in Oregon, and I was making serious headway with Sarah Wilson.

Let's start with a little background. I was shot by the nephew of a cartel drug lord we captured a few years ago. Gonzales, the nephew, is now serving time in the same federal facility that El Honcho, the drug lord, resides in. Gonzales and I crossed paths in an FBI sting I was involved in last year. The sting was breaking up a money laundering ring in Idaho that stretched to the East Coast.

One of the architects of this ring was Sydney Trocheck. He attempted to insnare my son-in-law, who at the time was knee-deep in laundering the East Coast mafia's ill-gotten gains. Sydney and my son-in-law flipped to become an FBI assets. It didn't hurt that Sydney was enamored with Dr. Susan Kenrick, the FBI's financial forensic expert. He was able to get limited immunity as long as he continued to work with Dr. Kenrick. The mafia was taken down, but a casualty was Jeffery. He was assassinated on the street by a mafia hit team.

The FBI had previously moved my daughter and the twins out-of-State for their protection. I took the lead on this protective move, moving them to Lakeview, Oregon ... for the second time. Sarah Wilson was an agent assigned by the FBI as part of Wanda's protection detail while Wanda was in New York City for Jeffery's funeral. Subsequently, she and I had something going on.

Now Lakeview, a town in eastern Oregon, is where I ended up several years ago when I was on the FBI's wanted list. That was a gross misunderstanding; the North Koreans were after me. During my stay in Lakeview, Sheriff Smith and my boss, Bill Anderson, at Eyeball Inc. conspired to keep me in Lakeview as a deputy sheriff. While there I helped disrupt a drug ring that killed my girlfriend, Suzie Wong. Samuel Horneck, one of Smith's informal deputies, watched my back when I went after the scum. I was out for revenge. We took the drug network down, and to everyone's relief, I didn't kill anyone. Samuel was later part of the team that helped capture El Honcho in Texas' Big Bend National Park.

A year later, Samuel and I led an extraction team to collect a terrorist mastermind from the mid-east. In response, his followers within the country targeted my family and me. While I was Lakeview's acting Sharrif (that's another story), I moved Wanda and the kids to Lakeview so I could watch over them. Bad planning, the terrorist found Wanda and the twins. After a

2

shootout: my team zero casualties, terrorists one dead, and two in custody. I ended up testifying before Congress about terrorist activities.

You may wonder what set off this chain of events. I'm Sean Murphy. I retired from the Army a half-decade ago. My former commanding officer, Colonel Bill Anderson, recruited me to work for him in his then-new company, Eyeball, Inc. We had a long history together as Army Rangers. I worked with him on several covert operations in Afghanistan and in Iraq. He was a field grade officer, and I was senior enlisted. We worked well together. His new company specialized in discreet services for the Government's alphabet agencies.

***

While getting a cup of coffee, Adam, the Colonel's righthand man joins me, asking how Wanda and the twins are doing now that she has decided to stay in Lakeview.

"Wanda opened a small financial investment service and is making a go of it. There is no competition. Jeffery's undeserved reputation helps bring in new customers, hoping she inherited insight into strategies that might not be available to the run-of-the-mill financial planners. Millie and Arnold have settled in and are doing well in school and sports."

About that time Henry and Butch take seats at the table. Adam assigned Henry, Butch, and Mark as my guardian detail when I was evading the North Koreans. They were ten years my junior and became known as my rottweilers. The rottweilers were part of the El Honcho takedown and later assisted in the extraction of Sa'd Ibn Atiq from Iraq. Henry and

3

Butch are former Navy SEALs, but we don't hold that against them. Mark was Army Special Forces.

"It's time you stopped malingering," said Butch. "An Army Ranger gets a little scratch and thinks he's entitled to sit on the beach for a few months."

"How is Mark doing?" He continued.

Mark was part of Wanda's protection detail. He was embedded in the Lakeview Sheriff's Office as a deputy and directed to keep an eye open for possible threats, i.e., East Coast mafia types. He went native. He liked the job, and more to the point, he liked a fellow deputy … Rebecca.

"Mark is as happy as a hog in mud. He and Rebecca plan to get married in the fall. You should be getting your invitations soon."

Turning the conversation to work, I ask Adam, "Where's the Colonel this morning? His car is not in his parking space."

"He went to DC to drum up new business. Knowing you were coming back, he wanted to line something up you could shoot at," Adam said with a smile. "No, seriously, he had two appointments this morning: one with DHS and the other with the RNC. I think they have something to do with the upcoming presidential primary."

2　Background

It was a fine-looking spring weekend. Trees were budding and the sky was blue. Sarah and I were finishing breakfast. I cleared the table as she stuffed the dishwasher. "What should we do today?" was the question.

Sarah was on Wanda's protection detail when I met her. Over the past several months she and I found we had much in common. We both lost significant others, me over a decade ago, and Sarah's loss was in the past five years. I had two grown kids; she had one. We both worked for law enforcement; me, in a roundabout way, as a contractor, she as an agent. We traded weekends; I'd spend a weekend with her in her Alexandria condo, and she'd reciprocate and spend a weekend at my Richmond apartment.

"How about the Cherry Blossoms," I said "the weatherman reported this morning the buds are just opening. We can stroll around the tourist attractions before tourists arrive."

About then my cell chirped. Looking at it, I saw I had a new text message from Anderson. Opening it up, I commented to Sarah, "Looks like I'll have a busy Monday after all;

Anderson wants my team and me in his office a nine. We have a new contract with the RNC."

Sarah looks at me with a concerned expression.

***

Early Monday morning I pulled my team together and over coffee, told them of Anderson's desire to see us.

"What's up?" asks Henry.

"A new contract. It's almost nine; let's head to the front office, Anderson can enlighten us."

As we settled around the conference table, Anderson quips, "Sean, why don't you get some coffee," noting I had my coffee mug with me. It had become an office joke; if you wanted to find Sean look for his coffee cup.

"Gentlemen, we have a new contract with the RNC. As you know, the presidential primaries are about to start. The RNC has several hopefuls, but three take top billing. A sitting senator, Senator Oscar Monroe from Oklahoma; a businessman from the Midwest, Willie Nelson, no not that Willie; and the sitting Governor from Virginia, Governor Martha Stillman."

"The RNC's concern is the possibility of disruptions. Senator Monroe has staked out some rather controversial; some would say extreme, positions. He's the far right's poster boy."

"Mr. Nelson, a prominent and successful businessman, is pushing for traditional fiscal restraint. He has broad support from both conservatives and some crossover liberals."

6

"Now the most interesting contender is Governor Stillman, a black female. A former marine. She is a longtime member of the Republican Party, has the female suburbia vote, and a healthy following in minority communities."

"The RNC chairwoman is concerned that each of these candidates will draw the wackos out of the woodwork. Our contract with the RNC is to monitor and eliminate threats to the candidates as they occur, and where possible, before they occur."

As Anderson pulls to closure, he looks at me, "Sean, you are Eyeball's lead on this. Let me know what support you need. I suggest you contact Agent Dillion to see what fringe groups the FBI is tracking. Also, here are contact details for the RNC, and for each presidential hopeful."

Later that morning I called Dillion. I don't need to look his number up; it's emblazed in my mind from last year. He answers on the third ring, "Dillion good morning. How are things in 'feebie' land?"

"I've been waiting for your call. I understand Eyeball has a new contract with the RNC. Now tell me, how do you plan to step on our toes?"

"Well, you obviously know more than I do. This is my first exposure to a presidential primary other than spin from the media. I think you know our proposed role, protect the candidates from the wacko fringes. Anderson suggested I touch base with you to get background information on some of these groups. And it goes without saying we will work with your people, sharing information, and occasionally conducting dark

7

operations your people might like but are constrained in conducting."

"We should get together," Dillion says. "How about Wednesday at the FBI lab in Quantico? I'll see you at ten." And then he disconnects.

Wednesday morning, Butch, Henry, and I are slogging north on I-95. "God, won't they ever get a handle on the rush-hour traffic" I'm thinking.

We're in the conference room with our coffee when Dillion walks in followed by two junior agents.

"Nice to see you again Sean," says Dillion. "Butch, Henry, good to see you both. I assume you're here to keep Sean out of trouble. Good luck on that."

"Okay, enough chit-chat. I've invited Agents Keith Foote and Johnny Dickerson to join us. Agent Foote is knowledgeable of fringe groups supporting liberal causes. Abortion, social and economic justice, etc. Agent Dickerson tracks the more challenging fringe groups: skinheads, neo-Nazis, and white supremacists. I wanted Agent Melinda Cox here this morning, but she is on maternity leave. She is our Black Lives Matter expert. But not to worry, she and Johnny collaborate with information on the more violent groups."

Dillon turns to the two agents and asks for their quick assessments,

Keith picks up the ball saying, "Senator Monroe has a history with issues important to conservatives. We expect antiabortion groups to protest at his events. The LGBT fringes

8

may join these protests. If the past is any measure of public response, protests against Senator Monroe will be loud, well attended, but mostly peaceful. The most physical threat will be a possible can of red paint."

"Mr. Nelson," Keith goes on, "will probably be the most ignored of the three. His passion for free trade, a responsible Fed, and a balanced budget have limited fringe group opposition since Occupy Wall Street went quiet. The one possible exception is Antifa. If they oppose Mr. Nelson, it could get violent."

"Governor Stillman," Johnny picks up, "will be a lightning rod. Although she is a traditional conservative, she will be attacked by fringe groups such as the Aryan Brotherhood, because of her race. Last week Melinda expressed some concern about BLM protests against the Governor because she is a conservative and viewed as an Uncle Tom, or whatever the proper term is for the female counterpart. In short, I think Governor Stillman may be the target of violent protests."

"I am not surprised by these assessments," I tell Dillion. "I am tasking Butch to Senator Monroe's campaign, Henry to Mr. Nelson's, and I will take point on Governor Stillman's campaign. And it goes without saying we will backfill for each other. Dillion, your team members can contact any one of us at any time."

We shared contact information and Keith and Johnny provided web links to various groups. They also provided printed copies of FBI in-house information on the groups and the group leaders.

This had the makings of a busy summer.

3 The RNC

I briefed Colonel Anderson on our meeting with Dillion and his people Thursday morning. After a short pause, he called in a couple of Eyeball's in-house analysts and assigned them to my team. I've worked with Caroline and Chloe on other projects and have always been amazed at the information they can tease from the internet.

"Okay Sean, get on with it," he said. "Keep me in the loop."

I asked Caroline and Chloe to meet with my growing team in fifteen minutes.

I swung by Butch and Henry's cubicles, told them of our new tech support, and asked them to join us in the conference room. "And bring any relative information you may have" I added.

"We are into day two of this assignment," I say to start the meeting. "We all know each other, so without more ado, here is where we are. We have three potential republican presidential candidates: Senator Monroe, Mr. Willie Nelson, and Governor Martha Stillman. Each is no stranger to the national spotlight. On the other side, we have BLM, the Proud Boys, Antifa, the Aryan Brotherhood, and other fringe groups. Our tasking is to keep the former safe from the latter."

"Here is how I would like to start. Caroline and Chloe immerse yourselves in the web, find out what you can about our players, and any intersections between team A, the good guys, and team B, the bad guys. Henry and Butch contact the campaign managers for your assigned candidates. Introduce yourselves and see what their concerns are. I will do the same for the Stillman campaign. Let's meet Monday morning at eight to exchange information. We can make Mondays a standing meeting."

"In the meantime, we will visit the RNC headquarters in DC. I called earlier this morning. They are hosting a security meeting for the candidate teams tomorrow and are eager to meet us. Butch, you can drive. Check out the Eyeball van this afternoon so we can leave at five in the morning. Mabey we can get ahead of the traffic."

***

"Five o'clock, who picked this time" I'm muttering.

We meet in the Eyeball parking lot. Butch has three very large coffees. "We'll need a pitstop by Woodbridge," mutters Henry.

Rush-hour traffic doesn't fail to impress. I think I-95 rents out parking space. But with all the delays we arrive at the RNC headquarters on 1st St. SE by nine. Henry and I get out as I say with a straight face, "Butch find a parking space, and we will meet you inside."

"Good luck with that" I'm thinking.

We're inside schmoozing while working the pastry table. It takes Butch about twenty minutes before he joins us. As I'm working on my second lemon danish, there's a tap on my shoulder. It's Sarah.

"Sean, what are you doing here?"

"And you?" I'm just as surprised to see her.

I gave her a 30-second recap of Eyeball's contract and my assignment to work with the Stillman campaign.

"Great," Sarah exclaims, "I'm on the FBI security team for Governor Stillman. What kind of conflict will this cause? One of us should ask to get reassigned."

"Let's not be too hasty; think of the positive aspects. It was only last week you were saying we should spend more time together" I quip with a smile. "But in all seriousness, this might be beneficial. Clearly, the Governor will be subject to threats, more so than the other candidates. Working together, a stealth collaboration if you will, we might be able to provide her greater security than either of us can on our own. Think about it."

"Well, I'll let it sit for now," Sarah says. "Here comes Ruben Holland, the Governor's campaign manager. Let me introduce the two of you, and no mention of our relationship."

After initial formalities, I tell Rubin about Eyeball's contract. "I'm here to identify and neutralize external threats before they occur. We have a team of people tracking fringe groups. They

13

work closely with the FBI's counter-terrorist team at Quantico. The FBI is providing your candidate with on-site security. That's Sarah's job. My job is to clear the landscape of threats."

"That's reassuring," Rubin says. "We've already received a handful of emails with various threats. I've turned them over to the FBI."

"We'll get copies. They'll help my team paint a landscape of the threat environment. I see the RNC's spokeswoman is starting to herd us into the conference room. She will, I'm sure, go over the security steps the RNC is taking. We can talk later."

The three of us enter the room. Sarah and Rubin sit at the conference table as I grab a back-row seat by the wall. Butch and Henry join me.

The spokeswoman welcomes all to the meeting. After going over the formalities, she introduces the people at the table. As she gets into the security overview segment, she emphasizes three areas: the candidates and their teams, be aware, be cautious, and don't be dumb. She mentions the FBI and the security details provided for each leading candidate. And finally, the she mentions RNC's contract with Eyeball to provide threat assessments and mitigation efforts. At that point, she nods to the three of us.

The confab breaks up in late afternoon. As we leave I tell Rubin we will be in touch and give him my card. "Call me at any time," I tell him. As I turn to Sarah as she whispers, "Not now; we'll talk this weekend."

Henry and I follow Butch back to the van. He's parked on the street two blocks away near Garfield Park.

"You think we'll have tires on the van when we get there Butch?".

"Funny, next time you drive."

4 Iowa State Fair

That weekend Sarah and I discussed our roles in the upcoming primaries. We agree to keep them separate in public; no need for public gossip. We will maintain a professional distance on the campaign trail as dictated by our respective jobs. Dillion will be told, but he already knows of our relationship and probably intended for our overlapping roles. It's the kind of thing he does. We will discreetly share information and rumors that may impact the Governor. With that decided, we settled in for one of our last weekends together until after the primary season.

We decide to go out for a final dinner. Susan suggests Bookbinder's, a swanky restaurant in an old tobacco warehouse just off the James River in Richmond's tobacco row district.

"Good choice," I say as I remember my last visit there when I met Ann, an old heartthrob and her 6-foot-6 husband, a Richmond police detective. My rottweiler had to intervene before Lt. Lugger of the Richmond Homicide Department ordered the giant to stand down. Lugger was investigating a

16

shooting in my condo complex. The complex manager had killed a North Korean agent who was sent to kill me. "Found memories," I'm thinking.

We have a great dinner, Sarah the seafood salad and me a man-sized steak. As we are lingering over coffee and cheesecake, who walks by our table, Governor Stillman.

She stops. "Agent Wilson, it's nice to see you. I'm glad to see you enjoying the evening. It'll probably be our last quiet one for the next few months."

She turns to me, "I believe you are Sean Murphy; Ruben has been telling me about you. Tell Colonel Anderson hello for me when you see him."

And with a wink, "I see my security is in good hands," she says as she walks to her table.

***

Its August and the candidates are headed to Des Moines for the Iowa State Fair. It's time to kiss some babies and eat questionable deep-fried food.

I've checked myself into the downtown Hampton Inn & Suites. It's located between the fairgrounds and the airport. It is also on the fringe of the cluster of upscale hotels in the city center.

The Governor and her entourage have checked into the Embassy Suites on the other side of the Des Moines River. Who knew Des Moines had a river? Stillman's FBI detail have also taken up residence there. Willie Nelson, his aide, and Henry, at Willie's invitation, are at the Des Moines Renaissance

17

Hotel, a hotel that caters to the city's business clientele. Senator Monroe's party has taken up residence at the posh AC Hotel by Marriott in the East Village, reflecting his deep-pocketed supporters. Butch has been relegated to the Econo Inn by the fairground.

Based on the Eyeball research team, various taverns have been identified where questionable characters may be found. Just for the hell of it, I head for Dave's Dive, a bar on the city's south side about fifteen minutes from my hotel. Its one redeeming feature is, it has none. If you want to be inconspicuous, this is the place. As I park, I notice several out-of-state plates in the parking lot; Idaho and Pennsylvania catch my interest.

I secure a stool at the end of the bar which gives me a good perch for people watching. There are about a dozen men, no women, spread between the bar and the booths. Three stand out, skinheads in their 20's and looking to be Aryan Nation fanciers. While sipping my beer, I surreptitiously take a half dozen pictures of them in their booth, as one makes a trip to the men's room, and a group shot as they are departing.

The bartender says to me as he's wiping the bar, "Those three are trouble. They arrived when the fair opened last week and have been in here a few times. I've caught pieces of their conversations. It sounds like they are planning some mayhem."

"Any idea where they are from?"

"Their cars have Idaho and Pennsylvania plates, kind of far afield to be hanging out in a place like this," the barkeep replies.

I thank him, finish my beer and head back to the Hampton Inn where I pull up my photo work. "Not bad," I think; there are a few shots providing good facial detail. I compose a quick note for Dillion and send the photos to him along with the license plate numbers I wrote down.

***

The candidates were out schmoozing by midday. Each had an assigned time for speeches. Nelson was first at one p.m. As he takes the stage someone is playing 'On The Road Again.' He promises economic reforms to get a handle on inflation and to create new jobs. He got a smattering of applause.

Next up was the Senator. He reiterated his opposition to abortion and pooh-poohed climate change. As predicted, there were several people there, appearing to be mostly college students with protest signs calling him a bigot and a sellout to corporate greed.

Governor Stillman took the stage midafternoon; she had the cleanup act. Her shtick was inclusiveness and fair elections. My three characters from last night were there and started yelling some not-so-nice things. As they started to threaten the stage, I saw Sarah step forward, placing herself between them and Stillman. The local police stepped in and, not too gently, removed the three from the fairgrounds.

The final event of the day was the deep-fried food challenge. The concoction offered, a favorite in Iowa's deep woods, deep-fried bacon on a stick wrapped around fatty chuck steak ... delicious.

Stillman looked at it, smiled, and graciously offered it to a nearby police officer thanking him for his earlier intervention. Looking at his fat on a stick, Nelson spent the next 15- or 20-minutes pontificating on Iowa beef. The crowd soon lost interest in what he did with it. Now the Senator, always out to please the crowd, gulped and took a bite. "I give him credit; he could keep it down."

Later that evening I got a text from Dillion. Subjects in my photos were identified as active members of the Aryan Brotherhood. Alexis, the youngest, was out of Idaho. Pete and Warren from the backwoods of Pennsylvania. All had extensive rap sheets. From what Dillion was able to find, it looked like Pete was the senior of the three; at least he had the longest rap sheet.

I headed back to Dave's Dive hoping they would be there. They were.

Walking up to the bartender and pointing to the three, "I'll take a beer and three more for my new friends."

He looks at me as if to say, "What the hell are you doing?"

I wink at him, and with the four bottles in hand, I squeeze into their booth, perhaps jostling Alexis a little to make room.

"I saw you today. It's time someone spoke out against that black bitch."

"And you are? they ask.

"A like-minded friend," I say as I sip my beer.

"Name is Alan, and you are Pete, Warren, and Alexis, members of the Brotherhood. A misunderstood organization if there ever was one."

"Who the hell are you!" Alexis blurts out.

"As I said, I'm a friend. My Americans Unite Organization is relatively new. Membership is restricted to more seasoned citizens, most with intelligence sources of a restricted nature or substantial personnel resources. Unlike the Brotherhood, which we view as shock troops, we prefer a more cerebral game. Now don't get me wrong, the Brotherhood is needed to confront our enemies, while AUO provides a structure and an end game. We should be working together."

Somewhat bewildered, Pete nods.

Getting up to leave, "Have a nice night," I say, "I expect to see you at some of the upcoming campaign events."

5 The Bus

The campaign is back on the road, literally. The Governor has rented a bus and is traversing Iowa. Willie, in his Gulfstream, has landed at almost all Iowan airports. The least active is the Senator. He has dispatched his minions to the hinterlands carrying his message of hope while he returns to Washington to filibuster.

I've talked with Sarah a few times, told her of my new 'friends' and how I plan to gain their trust. That plan hinges on Dillion. I've asked him to make some ripples in the rumor mill about the new Americans United Organization movement and its founder Alan Sloan. Alan is a secretive figure; no photos are available. AMO, a far-right group, is advocating a return to the Nation's founding ideals where the vote is restricted to male property owners. For census purposes, minorities will only be counted as three-fifths of a person as the constitution originally dictated.

There is only an occasional out-of-state rally; the candidates are focused on Iowa. The primary vote will occur in a few days. I spot my Aryan friends in Cedar Rapids. I congratulate them on their boorish actions and share a couple beers.

"You three appear to have slipped into the woodwork. I've only seen you at two rallies. Losing interest?"

"Warren's car broke down," says Pete, "and Alexis was called back to Idaho for a few days. Apparently, his people are not happy with him. They wanted us on the Des Moines Register's front page. And now we need to go to New Hampshire next week. Damn, we need money and better transportation."

"Life is tough," I say.

"What can AMO do for us? You said we were your shock troops. Let's have a little support."

Well now, this puts me in a tricky situation. Do I support these nuts and cause the Stillman campaign potential trouble? Or do I just sympathize with their plight and walk away?

"I need to talk with some of my associates. I'll get back to you. Give me your contact information."

"Man, I thought you knew all about us," says Warren.

"I do; your shoe size is 11 ½ D. But I need a reliable cell number that's off the grid. If you recall, I told you some of our members have intelligence sources. They know cells can be tapped. My people are picky."

They look at each other; Pete asks for a pen and writes a phone number on a napkin. "Okay, here is my cell number," he says as he pushes the napkin over to me.

Early the next morning I get Dillion and Anderson on a joint call and tell them where I am with respect to the skinheads.

Dillion quickly summarizes our position "How do we support them and not support them? I can see the Senate Oversight Committee going ballistic if we finance them, and I can see them walking if we do nothing."

"I have access to an old bus," says Anderson. "We could give it to them after we rig it with hidden mics and some remote-control mechanics."

"That's an interesting idea; we might even be able to pick up some useful information. How do we put this into play?" asks Dillion.

"I'll get Eyeball's people on it today with a target date of delivering the bus to Sean in Iowa in three days, just before the primary."

"Okay," says Dillion. "Sean, take $5 K and give it to them with the bus. Tell them it's to cover operational expenses."

Early that afternoon I called Pete and told him I had their transportation problem solved. He's to meet me at Dave's Dive in three days at about eight.

Eyeball is on schedule delivering the bus. It's dropped off Monday morning at the Big Barn Harley-Davidson Dealership just off I-80. The keys and paperwork are left with 'Bernie the Dealer,' a local TV personality. Turns out Bernard Oldfield served under Anderson years ago.

The bus is an old Greyhound Scenic Cruiser with domed windows on top. On the downside, it's a relic of the 1950s, or as some would say, it's vintage. But to its credit, it's in sound mechanical condition, and the interior is livable. In the late '90s, it was converted into a home on wheels for an up-and-coming Nashville star, Yodeling Bill Cody. After his star flamed out, the bus was relegated to the back corner of one of his fan's barns. With refreshed motor oil, new tires, and a tank of gas, the bus was ready to go.

Monday night I wheel the behemoth into Dave's parking lot, next to the Pennsylvania and Idaho plates. Entering the bar, I get a beer, locate the trio and join them.

As I drop the keys and envelope onto the table in front of Pete, I say, "He who asks receives. The keys are to the bus in the parking lot, and here is five thousand dollars to cover operational expenses."

As one, they get up and rush out. "That's awesome, man," says Alexis. "Does it run?"

Pete is a bit more nonplussed. "What are we supposed to do with that? My father talked about trips as a kid on dinosaurs like that."

"What the hell do you want for free? It gets you from point A to B, and as a bonus, it gives you a place to sleep. You have no imagination do you" I say. "Give me the keys and I'll get it out of here!" I say, perhaps too loudly, "and don't ask me for any more support."

In a circumspect voice, Pete agrees the bus meets their needs and reluctantly thanks me for it.

"Okay," I say. Tomorrow is caucus day. Make yourself useful, don't get arrested, and I'll see you in New Hampshire."

I Uber back to the hotel and report in with Anderson. "Bernie the Dealer sends his regards. Let me ask you," I say tongue in cheek, "who don't you know?"

The Iowa primary goes off as scheduled with only minor disruptions. It's reported on the evening news that some Aryan Brotherhood types clashed with a small Black Lives Matter contingent. Ironically both groups were protesting Governor Stillman.

Governor Stillman is the clear winner with twice the caucus returns as the runner-up, Willie Nelson.

6 Pennsylvania

'Larry, Moe, and Curly' take three days to reach Cross Fork, Pennsylvania. They abandon Warren's car in Dave's parking lot … after draining the last of the gas from its tank. Alexis follows in his car. The trip took three days. As they were passing Toledo on I-90, Alexis was pulled over for expired plates. Instead of meekly accepting the Trooper's ticket, Alexis goes off on him, calling him a charred Smoky, among other things..

Seeing Alexis pulled over, Warren pulls the bus onto the shoulder, and he and Pete walk back to help Alexis. What could go wrong? The Trooper, being approached by two skinheads and the third getting out of his car, pulls his gun and calls for backup.

Minutes later, two patrol cars, lights flashing and sirens blaring, arrive on the scene. The second coming from the opposite direction, cuts across the center strip in a cloud of dust. The first officer has the three face-down on the side of the road.

It takes the local judge a day before he schedules a bench hearing. The judge finds the only infraction of the law was the expired registration of Alexis's car. He impounds the car until the registration is fixed. He warns the three twits that they came close to being charged with willfully intimidating a law officer in the course of his duties. He lets them go with a warning and tells Alexis he can reclaim the car when he returns with an updated registration.

As the three climb aboard the bus which is parked in the next-door police parking lot, Alexis chuckles, "Those yokels now have a piece of shit on their hands."

***

The following morning the bus pulls into Cross Fork, Pennsylvania parking at Kinney's Country Store and Bar. Our three boys order a beer. Felix, the store's manager, says, "Pete, I haven't seen you in here recently; where have you been, and what is that pile of junk in my parking lot?

"Felix, stuff it," responds Pete. Has Otto been in recently?" I need to tell him I'll be bringing the bus up to the cabin. I don't want the boys getting trigger-happy."

Otto is a 40-year-old loser who has assumed leadership of the Pennsylvania chapter of the Aryan Brotherhood. The cabin is an old logging camp up in Barrel Slide Hollow. It was grandfathered in when the State purchased the Susquehannock State Forest in the late 19th century. There are usually two or three Aryans watching the old logging trail, Elk Lick Run, and they have been known to shoot at the tires of approaching vehicles.

Our boys return to the bus and head up Cross Fork Rd. to the logging trail. The bus has a tight fit navigating the old trail, but thirty minutes later it pulls into a cleared area next to an old house.

Otto and two of his minions are on the porch. "Where did you get that monstrosity" yells Otto.

"Don't bad mouth my hotel on wheels" yells back Pete. "It can sleep four, has a refrigerator for cold beer."

Our three heroes dismount the bus and join Otto on the porch. Warren goes into a long story about the bus's history, how it was once owned by Yodeling Bill Cody...

Otto almost chokes on his beer. "Who did you say? Yodeling Bill? That black bastard! You sleep in his bed? We should lock you in it when we burn it."

"Hold on," says Pete. "Yodeling Bill is long gone and the bus has been fumigated. Besides, it gives us transportation and a base for operations. We could have used it in Iowa instead of staying in a seedy motel that normally rents units by the hour. Unless you have something better, cut the crap."

Otto dispatches his two minions to check out the bus. They spend fifteen minutes going through the inside then they check the outside bodywork before firing up the engine. A half-hour later they are back on the porch reporting to Otto that they can find no bugs or tracking devices. And overall, it looks like a sweet ride.

Satisfied, Otto turns to Alexis. "I understand you were called back to Idaho to explain your, and by extension, my boys' lack of success. What's the problem?"

"Well, I'd say disunity in our ranks," says Alexi. "The three of us are cast in the midst of thousands and expected to cause a disruption. Members of other Brotherhood chapters failed to show up. We were outnumbered by porta-potty attendants. You and other chapter leaders need to motivate the troops."

"Don't get smart with me, boy," snarls Otto.

"He's spot on," says Pete, "unless you and your counterparts show some leadership, the Brotherhood is not going to make a difference."

After a bit more acrimony, the group climbs aboard the bus and heads to Deb's Cross Fork Inn for something to eat.

Sitting around the table with burgers and fries, Otto proclaims the bus needs a name. "I have just the name, 'Roderick's Express.'"

"What kind of name is that?" they ask.

"Roderick was the name of Nathan Bedford Forrest's favorite mount. What could be more fitting as we ride the bus into the fray to do battle" chuckles Otto.

***

I returned home to collect a fresh change of clothes and empty my mailbox. The mailbox is Rodger's job. Rodger, my landlord, is often forgetful, perhaps still traumatized from killing my North Korean assassins. While home, I swing by the Eyeball office to chat with Anderson.

"Sean, I'm thinking of pulling Butch and Henry. Willie and the Senator are not drawing much attention. Your thoughts?

"I think you are right. The Senator's greatest threat is the inside-the-Beltway pundits digging through his past. As for Willie, it's a toss-up. Some of his business dealings have drawn Antifa's attention, but up to this point, that group has been quiet. If you do pull them can you attach one of them to Sarah's detail? I've gone undercover as I try to milk the skinheads for information and have been avoiding Stillman's campaign."

"I'll ask for a volunteer. But on another subject, let's have some fun. As you know, we are monitoring the movement of the bus. It's currently on the road headed for Florida. It's just passed Woodbridge on I-95. I'm thinking of disabling it just north of Rocky Mount. They will have to call a tow service. I have a friend there that owes me a favor."

***

About three that afternoon Anderson flips the switch and the bus grinds to a stop.

"What the hell is wrong with this thing?" yells Otto. "We're stranded in the middle of nowhere."

Pete gets out, goes around back, and pops open the engine cowl. Unfortunately, he knows nothing about diesels. After wiggling a few parts and a further heated discussion with Otto, he pulls out his phone and calls a tow company. Thirty minutes later, a large tow truck pulls up, and an old black man emerges. He introduces himself as Carl Wiggins, the owner of the nearest reliable garage.

"Understand you boys have a bit of a problem," he says as Otto goes apoplectic.

"Hang in there Otto," Pete says. He's going to tow us to his garage and should have us back on the road by morning."

The bus is towed to *Wiggin's Fix-It-Shop*. As Carl is unhooking the bus, he takes a closer look at it. "This is Yodeling Bill Cody's old bus. I was part of Yodeling Bill's entourage back in the day. I was responsible for this baby. How'd you boys get it?"

Every time Carl referred to the four Aryans as 'boys' it puts Otto on the edge of a stroke. One would think Carl is doing this deliberately.

"The motel next door is clean and cheap. It's run by my daughter." You could tell by Otto's expression he'd rather spend the night sleeping in the cornfield. "She also runs a fine restaurant." Let me get to work on your vehicle" said Mr. Wiggin as he rambles back into the garage.

Our four 'boys' toughed it out, Otto sleeping on the floor. They humble themselves and have eggs and toast at *Wiggin's Egg and Things Restaurant*. Pete and Warren are delighted with the food, and Alexis, somewhat more subdued, eats what's in front of him. Otto, on the other hand, sulks in the corner with his coffee.

About eight-thirty Carl comes in and announces, "Your bus is ready boys. You had some air in the fuel line. The diesel fuel is questionable. If you like, I can drain and replace it. Probably cost you around $300 for the fuel. My bill at this point is $135 for labor."

The boys decline the offer of fresh fuel and depart in a cloud of dust.

Carl is chuckling as he picks up the handpiece of an old dial phone and dials a number. "Colonel, it went off without a hitch. Never seen such an uptight bunch of skinheads. I reset the cutoff switch as you asked and they are now on their way."

"Thanks Carl, I owe you one," Anderson says with a laugh as he disconnects.

7 Florida

The candidates have a busy week crisscrossing the State, from Tallahassee to Miami. The primary is six days away. This year Florida is nudging out New Hampshire with the first primary election leaving only a week between the two primaries. The Governor has chosen to spend her time in Florida. Willie Nelson, with his corporate jet, is splitting his time between the two States. The Senator's campaign, on the other hand, is losing steam. He has only scheduled two events in Florida, paid for by his PAC, and one in New Hampshire. It looks like it is getting down to a two-person race.

I find Pete and company hold-up in a cheap motel by Jacksonville International Airport. "Otto, this is Alan Sloan. He's the one who gave us the bus."

"Such a gift," Otto says. "What's in it for you?"

"I take it your boys didn't Americans United Organization."

"In fact, they did, and I did a little google research. AMO is identified as a new group. Its aim is to restore constitutional norms. So, what does that do for us?"

"Well, other than material support, we have the same goals. You don't want Stillman; we don't want Stillman. Where we part ways, and as yet to be announced, we will support a third-party candidate. You will support a Nazi candidate in the general election. Neither of these candidates has a chance of being elected. A third-party contender may be able to influence the winning party's platform and possibly influence a few down-ballot races. Your choice, not so much. But as for the RNC primaries, neither of us want a viable presidential candidate like Stillman."

"Now it feels you are a bit hostile. I had some information to share with you but, UP YOURS; I'm out of here." I say as I turn for the door.

Otto, a bit taken aback, "Okay, I'm sorry I came on too strong. I'm always suspicious of new people. Let's get a beer and talk."

After comparing backgrounds and political objectives, I get to the point. "My sources tell me that BLM members from Atlanta will be at Stillman's upcoming rally. Apparently, they want to upstage the Brotherhood. There will be twenty or thirty schwarzermann, some with weapons. Their hidden goal is to intimidate and discredit the Brotherhood."

"How many men do we have?" Otto asks Alexis

"Besides us, we have about ten from Atlanta and a few from Alabama."

"That's good," says Otto. "Any chance of getting the Florida chapter to participate."

"I'm told they are holding their members in reserve for Miami."

"That's bullshit!" fires back Otto. "Tell them to get their asses over here."

***

The Governor's rally is scheduled to be held in three days at the University of North Florida in Hodges Stadium. Otto can field a few dozen foot soldiers. Not to be outdone BLM has amassed a respectable number of counter-protestors. Now to be clear, the counter-protest is against the Brotherhood; BLM is as opposed to Stillman's conservative positions as is the Brotherhood. But the opportunity for a faceoff with the Aryans on cable news ... priceless.

That night I call Dillion with my report. "The Brotherhood is planning to disrupt the Governor's rally. I provided him the information on the plans to quash BLM. The Aryans are arming themselves, planning an assault on BLM that will have prime-time viewers mesmerized."

"I'll have my people record it if it happens; perhaps we can justify a few arrests," says Dillion. "But that is not our goal. We want to quell any violence before it occurs. I have a man in the Atlanta BLM contingent. I'll ask him to contact you tomorrow, and perhaps the two of you can find a way to de-escalate the pending mayhem."

Next, I called Sarah and told her to steel herself for a challenging day. "It is my guess there is going to be total chaos tomorrow. I suggest you wear your vest and stay close to the Governor."

Around ten the next morning I get a call asking if I'm Alan. I need to stop for a moment to think about which identity I'm using this week. "Yes," I finally say.

"Dillion suggests we meet. Does this afternoon work for you?"

"Yes, let me suggest the Palm Plaza Café at the Jacksonville Zoo. I doubt if any of our associates will be in the area. 2 p.m.?"

"Works for me," the voice on the line says, and the line goes dead before I can ask him how I'll recognize him.

I get to the zoo at about one and walk around. Looking at some of the animals, I think several of my current associates would look good in these cages. I find the Café, take an outside table in a shaded corner and order coffee. At two, the assigned time, a huge black man, bald, with a full beard and wearing aviator sunglasses, sits down opposite me."

"It's been a while Sean; how ya doing?"

I'm trying to place this guy; I'm thinking I've never seen him before, then from the recesses of my mind, the voice is familiar.

"Jacob, what the hell are you doing here?" It was a little over a year ago that I worked with the FBI, Jacob as the lead agent, in pulling down a mob money laundering ring.

"Dillon thought I needed a little time in the sun, so he had me infiltrate BLM. Big Bear was more rational than these yahoos."

37

"Hope you're enjoying it. I'll trade my jackasses for your yahoos," I tell him with a smile. "Dillion wants us to calm the waters between the Brotherhood and BLM for the upcoming rally. How do we do that?"

"Without discrediting our covers, I have no idea. I didn't bring my magic wand."

"The only common goal between the two, is that Stillman does not become the republican's candidate. Can we build on that? I ask.

"It's worth a try."

After a little more chit-chat, Jacob leaves. I wander back to Otto's Motel 6 accommodations. My efforts to get him to focus on tomorrow's goal, discrediting Stillman rather than a confrontation with BLM, seems to be taking hold.

***

The Governor's rally is scheduled to be held Wednesday in Hodges Stadium. Jacob and I are hoping that by emphasizing common goals BLM and the Brotherhood will behave. Dillon is counting on us.

At 3:17 pm, mayhem breaks out in Hodges Stadium. The blacks and the skinheads have taken control of the field. A couple gunshots have Stillman supporters scrambling for the exits. The Governor's FBI detail has whisked Stillman away in a black SUV. Sarah was nearly trampled in the rush to secure the candidate.

The FBI, not counting on Jacob and my efforts, had a bunch of agents present. There were also state and city police present. Between them, they arrested twenty-two rioters: ten Aryans, and twelve BLM members, as well as confiscating three 9MM pistols.

Later that night I'm asking Otto what happened.

"That idiot from Idaho called one of those black bastards a 'f...ing black shit.' He didn't take it well and laid Alexis out, one punch mind you. You'd think Alexis would have had better sense than confronting the biggest buck in the herd. Then it went downhill. Alexis is in the hospital with a broken jaw, and Pete, with three of our people, are in a holding cell downtown."

"What a f...ing shit show."

"Well Otto, get a hold of yourself; we still have the Governor's rally this Saturday at the Villages."

8 The Villages

That night I get a call from a pissed-off Dillion. He has Anderson on a conference line.

"Sean, you and Jakob couldn't be trusted to keep a bunch of Boy Scouts away from a neighboring Girl Scout camp. If I wanted mayhem, I could have sent in union organizers. Good job!!!?

"On the upside," Anderson interjects, "the FBI got great press coverage. That clip of FBI agents rushing the Governor off stage and into the support vehicle will be played for years. And you got twenty-two scumbags off the street. All-in-all, a good day's work."

"Okay, it wasn't all bad," admits Dillion. "What surprise have you lined up for us at The Villages?" asks Dillion.

"Otto and company are licking their wounds but plan on making a statement this Saturday. I expect a dozen or so skinheads to show up."

"Sean, a heads up," says Anderson, "I plan to be at The Villages this weekend. My old boss, General West, has invited me down. He and a few other former Rangers are getting together. You are welcome to join us if it doesn't blow your cover."

"Oh great, we have you and Jacob struggling to manage your charges and now a bunch of cowboys in their golf carts. What could go wrong?" sighs Dillion.

The boys fire up Roderick's Express and head to the Lake Mary Campground on the edge of Ocala National Forest. The campground is not far from The Villages. Several of the skinheads came to Florida on their motorcycles and are staying at a nearby rent-by-the-hour motel. Otto and Warren, Pete is detained in Jacksonville, are getting around in Warren's car which was towed by the bus.

To maintain my cover, I am staying at the Holiday Inn Express & Suites, one of the more expensive hotels in the area, only $147 a night.

***

General West has one of the more modest 4,000 sq. ft. retirement homes. There is a massive screened-in deck overlooking the lake. He is hosting about two dozen retired Rangers. His driveway looks like a golf cart showroom. There are your basic models up to those with enclosed cabs with air conditioning. Most are electric, but a few have small four-stroke engines; a couple are chopped VWs. One is decked out as Cruella De Ville's car down to the exhaust ports.

The geriatric set is talking about Wednesday's riot in Jacksonville and how they wished they were there. All plan to attend the Governor's rally Sunday and hope for a repeat.

Anderson and I are sitting on the sidelines, listening to the boasts. The General comes over. "Sean, I don't know if you remember me, but we've met a couple times over the years, mostly when I was pinning medals on your chest. The Colonel here has always had good words for you, and I've followed your career. Drug lords, mafia, North Korean assassins ... you'd have been safer staying in the Army."

"Colonel Anderson has always had a way of keeping me busy," I respond.

"Ya, I know. Now you are covertly working for the FBI, I believe. Are we going to have any excitement tomorrow?"

"I don't know what the Colonel's been telling you, but we're hoping for a noneventful rally."

"Well, we will see," the General continues. "Has Colonel Anderson ever told you about his early days in the Army? Let me tell you about when I first met him."

Anderson starts to blush. This must be a good story.

It was in the early 70s when our active involvement in Vietnam was winding down. I was a major with the 1st Cavalry Division when we got an allotment of new officers. One was a butter bar[1], still wet behind the ears. Given active engagements were dwindling, I thought I'd do him a favor and assign him to one of our forward bases. Give him a chance for some real experience before we dee-dee maowed[2] out of the country.

---

[1] a slang reference for a Second Lieutenant
[2] (dee-dee maow": Vietnamese for "go away fast" or "haul ass")

Well, he was with the company for about a week when he was sent out on patrol. His commanding office sent a seasoned noncom to keep him out of trouble. Our intrepid 2nd Lieutenant put the noncom at the end of the file and ignored him. An hour or so into their patrol, they came to a small hamlet. The Sargent tried to tell the Lieutenant this was a friendly village. There were reports of Viet Cong on the south side of the village. The patrol should skirt around the village to take them out.

Our Lieutenant said to hell with that; he was going into the village to find the headman. He formed up the men and headed across a small bamboo bridge when all hell broke out. It sounded like bedlam, flashes of white all around the Lieutenant. The other men had held back at the Sergeant's direction, leaving the Lieutenant exposed. Some of the men almost wet themselves laughing so hard. The Lieutenant pulled his service weapon and starts indiscriminately firing; he's scared shitless. The Sargent steps forward, fires a short burst into the air from his M-16 getting the Lieutenant's attention, and orders him back.

The Sargent congratulates the Lieutenant on killing three enemy geese. He explained the White Mice[3] used geese instead of dogs. They make

---

[3] (White mice: the Vietnamese national police force. Its members wore white

43

more noise, are more territorial, and cost less to keep.

The next morning our Lieutenant files insubordination charges against his platoon sergeant. A day or so later, the charges came to my attention. I have them both brought to my office. I asked the Lieutenant what happened. He tells me his story, and it's all I can do to keep a straight face. I asked him who he thought was in charge of the patrol. Him of course. BS, I tell him. He was there to learn. I told him seasoned sergeants are junior officers' strongest asset. Listen to them.

The villagers filed a claim for the three geese, $50 each. I told the Lieutenant he was responsible for paying the claim. Later we learned the villagers had a feast with the geese Anderson killed. We christened this as 'Anderson's roast goose' feast.

"From then on, our Lieutenant matured into a capable officer," *the General said as he finished his story.*

I asked what happened to the platoon sergeant.

Anderson somewhat quietly says, "He was killed a month later. We were ambushed, I was wounded and unconscious. He took charge and called in a medevac for me and the three others who were down. He and two others held Charlie at bay while we were secured. As the medevac lifted off, the three

---

shirts)

44

dove into the door. Sargent Chesterfield was hit in the back. He didn't make it."

***

Sunday's rally was held at the Club House. The Governor, a former marine, was held in high regard by the community, even those supporting the opposition party. She was scheduled to speak in midafternoon. There was a large gathering around the stage, and many more attendees in gulf carts parked around the edges.

Shortly after Stillman started her campaign speech, the Aryan Brotherhood made its appearance. Some on motorcycles, others marching carrying ugly banners. Cable news crews were zooming in on them and then flipping back to the stage. As the senior warriors formed a wall of walkers around the stage, an air horn blared. The gulf carts moved forward in a pincer movement cutting the skinheads off. The only opening was to retreat. In this confusion, the golf cart decked out as Cruella De Ville's ride charged into the Aryans as if it was a member of the light brigade. Its exhaust pipes were more than decorative, 3-ft flames were shooting out. The Brothers ran in full retreat. Cable news, even those opposed to the Governor, carried this footage for weeks.

9 New Hampshire

On to New Hampshire.

I'm staying at Manchester's Double Tree Hotel. My Aryan friends have found a campground near Bear Brook State Park with the overflow staying at Big Al's Motor Court. "Damn, this place makes the Wiggins Motel look good," observed Otto.

The Governor's campaign had a few days to catch up with Willie, and poll results were looking good.

The Saturday before the primary, Stillman was at the Red Arrow Diner in Manchester behind the counter, serving breakfast to all comers. She is wielding a mean spatula and could flip pancakes with the best of them.

Her FBI detail was in a tizzy with town folks coming and going. When Otto and Warren wandered in, she served them each a '4 stack' with bacon. When I entered the restaurant, Sarah looked at me and rolled her eyes. I joined the line at the counter; I only got a 3-stack. I took my tray and joined Otto and Warren in the corner booth. I waved to the waitress and asked for coffee.

Otto's first words were, "Look at all these rubes cozying up to that black bitch. We need to get her out of the race."

"And how are we going to do that?" whispers Warren.

"She could just disappear!" snarls Otto.

"Hold it, I'm not going there," I say as I start to get up.

"Sit down, don't get your undies in a wad," says Otto, "I'm just spouting off."

"But more seriously, how can we get her to drop out? We've been searching her history and can find no dirt. She has no vices, at least that we know of. Her husband is squeaky clean. My god, if she weren't black, you'd think she was June Cleaver. Her tenure as Virginia's Governor resulted in a balanced budget, a functioning political party, and a 67 percent approval rating. Damn, listen to me; you'd think I was going to vote for her."

"We have a real dilemma," I say. "My AMO movement is also stymied. Tell you what Otto, I have to go and see some people. I'll catch up with you later."

As I'm walking out, I flash Sarah a smile. Part way down the block, I call her cell.

"Did you get your pancakes?" I ask. If this doesn't work out, the Governor could do good as a short-order cook."

"Funny, the only thing she's flipping are votes. What do you want? I can't talk long."

"If you can break free this afternoon, I'll be at the City Library. Since I'm here, I thought I'd look at their genealogical records to see what I can find on my Scotch-Irish side of the family. They settled somewhere around here in the early 18th century."

That afternoon I'm engrossed in the colonial history of New Hampshire, where I find references to my relatives. It appears some were fleeing the Crown, malcontents who did not share the king's religious views. The group's patriarch, Reverend Hugh McGee, founded the first Presbyterian church in Londonderry, NH in 1717. The McGee's were on my mother's side of the family, removed by about four generations. Shortly after Lexington, a distant relative, Captain Elijah McGee raised a company and fought at Breed's Hill during the siege of Boston.

I'm engrossed in my research when I feel a tap on my shoulder. Looking up, there is Sarah.

Pecking her on the cheek, I say, "I didn't think you'd make it. Let's grab that cubicle by the window."

"I can only stay for a few minutes while the Governor takes a nap. We're staying at the Hilton, only a short walk from here. The Governor was impressed by your friends this morning," she says with a grin.

"Just a heads up," I tell Sarah. "Otto and some of his buddies, including two new malcontents, are planning something. When I entered the bus yesterday, they all clammed up, looking like a dog who just ate crap."

10 Snatched

Governor Stillman had a successful rally, good turnout. Students for the GOP from Dartmouth College had several hundred students there supporting the Governor.

It was about eight in the morning when I got a phone call from Governor Stillman's campaign manager, Ruben Holland. "Sean'" he starts, "I know your relationship with Sarah is hush-hush, but she told me to call you if anything out of the ordinary happens. Both Sarah and our press secretary appear to be missing. I just checked their rooms, and neither of their beds has been slept in. No one has seen them since after the rally."

"Ruben, call the State Police and report a potential kidnapping. Also, contact the FBI and let them know of a potential missing agent."

As the line is disconnecting, I'm speed-dialing Dillon.

"Sean you are up early. What can I do for you?" he says in a sleepy voice.

"Dillion, I think the Brotherhood has kidnapped Sarah and Stillman's press secretary. The secretary, Martha McGuinn, is a twenty-three-year-old graduate student from Old Dominion." I went on to repeat what Ruben had just told me.

"Okay, got it," Dillion says, now fully awake. I'll mobilize our people."

Within the hour the FBI issued an alert throughout New England for all authorities to be on the lookout for the kidnapped victims. Their descriptions were provided:

> Sarah Wilson, female in her early 50's, 5 ft 8 in, 130 pounds, with chestnut brown hair.
> Martha McGuinn, female mid-20's 5 ft 6 in, 110 pounds, with blond hair in a ponytail.

There was also a description of the bus they may have been abducted in, a vintage 1950s tour bus.

After my call to Dillion, I alerted Anderson to the abduction. He told me to do whatever was necessary. I called Henry, who was in town with Willie's campaign, and together we went to the campground where the bus had been parked. A quick discussion with the campsite manager revealed the bus left with no notice the previous night about ten. At Big Al's Motor Court, we found that the Aryans had decamped yesterday.

A little after eleven Dillion calls back. "Sean, we found the bus in York, Maine using the tracker Anderson had installed. It appears to have been abandoned by the York Harbor fishing docks. The night watchman there reports seeing it pull up about three in the morning and a half dozen people disembarking. They boarded one of the older fishing trawlers, which quickly pulled away from its berth and headed downriver. My people are working with other agencies to see if they have satellite images that might help."

Later Henry and I went to the Hilton where the Stillman campaign was staying, and started interviewing campaign members as well as hotel staff. The most frequent responses we got were

"I already told the State Police what I know."
"Why are you asking me again?"
"Who are you?"

The Governor was in the hotel lobby and invited us to join her and Rubin in the alcove she had appropriated.

"Sean, can you tell me what is going on?

"Governor, it appears the Aryan Brotherhood kidnapped your press secretary and Sarah sometime last night. The bus the Brotherhood was using, probably used in the abduction, was found this morning in York. A group of people from the bus were seen boarding a fishing trawler about three this morning. The FBI has been engaged, and I'm waiting for a call from Agent Dillion. I also talked with Anderson this morning; Eyeball will provide whatever is necessary."

It was then that the campaign manager received a call on his private cell; it was Martha. She wanted urgently to talk with the Governor. As Stillman took the phone, a male voice said, "We have your people. They will be fine as long as you do what we tell you. You are to announce you are dropping your presidential bid. This announcement is to be aired on CNN tomorrow evening at six," and the connection went dead.

For the next couple hours we had no new information. Governor Stillman invited us to stay with the campaign team as she talked with the FBI, but Henry and I retreated to my hotel where we made 'what if' plans. We had no idea where the trawler was headed.

In the early afternoon Anderson calls. "Sean, we found their location using NSA satellite imaging data. But there is a problem. They are in Nova Scotia; specifically, they are in West Green Harbor. The State Department is dragging its feet; they don't want an international incident. The FBI is in discussion with the Canadian Mounties, but nothing is moving fast."

Anderson continues, "I have a friend in Portsmouth with a fast boat that can get you to Nova Scotia tonight. I've dispatched Butch with night combat gear for you and Henry. He will meet you at the Kittery Point Yacht Yard at eight tonight.

"Thanks," I say, "let's keep Dillion out of this for now."

"Use some caution Sean; I don't want to bail you out of a Canadian jail."

Henry and I are in Portland by seven. As we are parking Butch comes across the parking lot "Thought you'd never get here," he says with a grin. "You gotta see our ride!"

We Walk out to the end of the pier, and there is a PT Boat. "What the hell, we exclaim!"

An ol' salt is sitting in the back of the boat. As he gets up to greet us, he says, "She's a beauty. Had her built-in 2016 for JFK's 100th birthday celebration, a recreation of his PT 109. It was a big hit in Hyannis. With a modern engine and new hull technology, I've increased its range by 30 percent and speed by 10 percent over the original. I'm Philip Boswell, CEO of

Boswell Maritime Repairs. Bill Anderson called this morning and told me of your predicament. Understand we are planning a quick trip to Nova Scotia tonight. Get aboard and let's get going."

11 West Green Harbor

It was just after eleven as we skirted the southern tip of Nova Scotia. The onboard GPS showed West Green Harbor thirty-five miles to the Northeast. Our craft was going about twenty-five knots. Anderson's satellite intelligence placed the kidnappers in an old cabin on the west side of the peninsula, a remote location.

Phill suggested we anchor the boat about a mile offshore. He told us to get the inflatable raft and compressor out of the front cabin, said we would be using it to go ashore.

We got the sucker inflated and launched it on the far side of the boat to muffle its splash as it went into the water. The three of us got in and started paddling for shore. "Where's the f...ing engine" I was muttering to myself. Butch told me to shut up and stop splashing my oar. "Sound travels over water," he whispered.

As we pulled close to the dock, Butch and Henry slipped over the side and made for the dock. "Well, I guess Navy SEALs do have their place," I thought.

Ten minutes later, I see the green signal light and paddle the raft up to the dock. On the dock, there are two trussed bodies. "Not to worry," says Butch, "they're alive, just taking a long nap."

At the house, we heard voices. Peeking in the front window, I could see three skinheads. One was Warren. It sounded like two more back in the kitchen area. One was yelling out, "I want the perky little blond … she's been waiting for me!"

Warren replies, "Keep your hands offer, at least for now. If Stillman doesn't come through, you can have her after me."

Butch comes up in back of me. "The hostages are in the back bedroom. They are hog-tied on the bed."

"Okay, here's the plan," I say. "Butch, you go to the back of the house and shoot anyone who comes into that room. Henry and I are going in the front door. Henry, if anyone of them lifts a gun, shoot them."

As we bust through the front door, as I expected, two grab their assault rifles, and Warren pulls out his Glock. After the initial burst of fire, the room is quiet. I could hear the back door slam as the two in the kitchen vacated the premises. I head to the back bedroom door. "Butch, it's me. I'm coming in." As I'm cautiously opening the door, Henry emerges from the kitchen. "Two ran into the woods," he says. "It would have been like shooting fish in a barrel, so I let them go."

At the sound of gunfire, Phill brings his PT Boat up to the dock with its spotlight trained on the cabin.

We untie Sarah and Martha. Other than some bruises, they are shaken up but physically fine. We help them to the front of the house, stepping over two bodies when I see Henry's been shot, a grazing round to the ribs. Sarah takes charge and stops the bleeding.

Looking down, I see Warren is still breathing. He's been shot in the chest and is probably bleeding internally. I kneel down beside him and ask, "Where is Otto?"

He wheezes, "This was all his idea."

"Where is he?" I ask again

As Warren is gasping his last breath, he says, "Pennsylvania."

It's about two in the morning as we return to the dock. Phill has loaded our two trussed skinheads and secured them in the stern of the boat. He helps Henry board, gets us seated, returns to the captain's chair, and is pulling away from the dock as a Canadian Coast Guard vessel appears, blue lights flashing, and over its loudspeaker, orders us to kill the engine.

A smile spreads across Phill's face as his left-hand hammers the throttle to its max. Within a second the front third of the PT Boat is out of the water. The boat shoots out of the inlet at max speed, and the blue flashing lights recede into the distance.

Two hours later, as the sun is rising, we are approaching Booth Bay Harbor. "Your boss, Colonel Anderson, said he'd meet us here," Phill says over his shoulder. Phill heads to a small dock on the far side of the cove. "Okay kids, the ride is over; Anderson will collect you here."

A half-hour later three SUVs pull up. Anderson gets out and, as he gets close says, "A successful trip, I take it."

"We have a peace offering for Dillion," I say as Butch points to our two captives. "Perhaps he can get some information out of them."

We load into the SUVs and head down I-295. After giving him a full account of the night's activities, I drift off into dreamland. When I wake up, we are pulling into the Hilton parking lot in Manchester. We take Martha up to her room. She is still in shock from the past thirty-six hours. I asked Stillman's campaign manager to stay with Martha for a bit.

Anderson, Sarah, and I are sitting in the Governor's campaign alcove. Anderson and Stillman have their heads together planning the campaign's next move. The story the campaign will put out is two campaign members were kidnapped by the Aryan Brotherhood. They were quickly recovered by the Governor's security team. Queries from the press will be ignored until the FBI can make an official statement. The campaign will continue as if nothing happened.

"Okay, I need to call Justin," Stillman says. I think we've ruffled some Canadian feathers."

She calls her office back in Virginia and asks them to get the Canadian Prime Minister on the line. A few minutes later her phone chirps, and she places it on speaker. "Justin, this is Kate Stillman; we met last year at the North American

57

Economic Conference. Before we talk further, I have you on a speaker phone with Bill Anderson."

"Kate, yes, I remember you and Bill; it's been some time since we went fishing. When will you be up here again?

"Perhaps we can try next spring in Nova Scotia when the salmon are running, that is, if you are still talking to me," Anderson responds. "I expect your staff has reported some dead bodies at West Green Harbor this morning and an irate Coast Guard Commander."

"As you may know, some people from the Governor's campaign were kidnapped two days ago by the Aryan Brotherhood. Their goal was to force her to drop out of the race. They took the hostages to Nova Scotia. When we tracked them down by satellite, the FBI contacted your Mounties. Our State Department became involved, and as you can guess, there was no short-term resolution. Some acquaintances took matters into their own hands and retrieved the hostages. I think they left a few bodies behind. Given that they are American bodies, you can ask our State Department to collect them."

"Now, to my main point, the FBI would like to avoid an international incident. I can see the headlines in the NYT now.

INTERNATIONAL TERRORIST PLOT TO UNDERMINE US ELECTIONS. SUSPECTS SEEKING REFUGE IN CANADA.

The cover story I propose is that the Mounties, working with the FBI, recovered the hostages who were safely freed and are back home. And to soothe their feelings at being left out, the Mounties can embellish the story as they like.

"Anderson, just like I remember you, always a convincing argument. Let me get with my people, and I'll get back to you. And I look forward to our fishing trip."

"Governor, are you still there? I'm looking forward to addressing you as Madam President next year."

12 Fallout

The next morning the Mounties release a press announcement:

> The Nova Scotia RCMP Detachment, working with the American FBI, secured the release of two hostages being held by the Aryan Brotherhood. The Brotherhood had hoped to force Governor Stillman to drop out of the American Presidential race.
>
> This is a further example of cross-border cooperation between our Nation's top law enforcement agencies.

New Hampshire's primary election was held the following Tuesday. On the GOP side, Governor Stillman was the hands-down winner. Senator Monroe was a no-show. His campaign team was, at this point, nonexistent. Willie Nelson graciously conceded and announced his support for the Virginia Governor, perhaps angling for a cabinet position.

Even as she was receiving congratulatory emails, her team was folding the campaign tent and moving on to South Carolina; there were only three months to the general election.

The goal now was to build bipartisan support for Governor Stillman.

The Eyeball team was back in Virginia licking its wounds, more specifically, Henry playing his 'flesh' wound to the fullest. Dillion suggests we could relax our coverage of Stillman for the time being. He also switched out the FBI's team covering the Governor.

Sarah and I were planning a quiet weekend at Sky Meadows State Park. I had scored a cabin rental which was exceedingly hard to come by this time of year. And then Dillion called.

"Sean, we are planning a little takedown party this weekend and thought you would like to assist. As a matter of fact, we need your assistance since you know the target. As a courtesy, I've put Sarah on the takedown team. Our target is Otto, and we believe he is holed up in a cabin just outside Cross Fork, Pennsylvania. You're familiar with the area I think?"

"Dillion, Sarah, and I had a quiet weekend planned. You owe me!"

"The team is assembling at an FBI field office in western Pennsylvania. We've secured a block of motel rooms, not that we will be there that long. Do you need transportation?" Dillion asks.

"No, Sarah and I will drive up. A hell of a letdown from a weekend together to a three-hour drive together ."

61

When we arrive at the field office, we are directed next door to a large garage where a dozen or so people are checking out equipment and getting final directions. By six, we are all set. Dillion points us to a diner across the street and tells us we can eat there, but otherwise, we are restricted to the area. The Super 8 Motel is next door where a block of rooms has been reserved. He advises us to get a good night's sleep; we will be on the road at 3 a.m.

At zero dark thirty, six FBI SUV's are on the road. I am with Dillon in the lead vehicle.

"Sean, that was one hell of a stunt you pulled up in Nova Scotia. It could have resulted in an international situation with Canada."

"But it didn't, and the FBI, without doing anything, came out smelling like a rose, and with two suspects to question."

"Tell me how you pulled it off," Dillion starts to say, but then, "no, don't, it's better I don't know."

The convoy blows past Cross Fork and turns up the logging road to Barrel Slide Hollow. A half mile from the cabin, the convoy stops, and Dillion waves the team to their preassigned positions.

Once everyone is in place, Dillion and I drive up to the front of the cabin. As I'm going up the front steps, Otto steps out.

"Alan, what are you doing here, and who's your friend?"

Our earlier thermal scan of the building showed three people.

"Otto, please ask your two friends to come out."

"What the hell is this," he says as he backs toward the door.

"If you want to get out of this alive Otto, get on your knees now! There is an FBI SWAT team surrounding the cabin."

A windowpane is shattered by a rifle barrel; I dive to the side, and all hell breaks loose. Otto is on his knees as the cabin is raked by automatic fire. The SWAT team moves forward, finds two bodies inside, and puts Otto in zip ties.

As Dillion and Sarah approach, I am saying "Otto you're one of the dumbest shits I ever met. You kidnap an FBI agent, then hide out here? You don't think they'll find you?"

Otto is taken into custody. During his interrogation he offers up Brotherhood supporters in the hope of a plea deal.

After some further questioning and conferencing with his lawyer, Otto claims one of the well-known social media moguls is funding the Brotherhood.

Dillion hops on this. "And what proof do you have Otto?"

"There is a small safe in the cabin, buried under the back bedroom floor. It contains my financial records."

Dillion dispatches his people and late that evening receives a call; they recovered a small safe just where Otto said it would be.

The next morning Dillion, Otto, and Otto's lawyer are in the interview room. The safe is brought in, and Otto is asked to open it. To open it requires Otto's thumbprint.

Otto, with his lawyer's consent, opens it. Dillion pulls out a ledger and some other papers. The ledger documents thousands of dollars transferred into Otto's bank account from an unidentified source. "Who's it coming from, Otto?" asks Dillion.

"Look at the document in the envelope."

Dillion opens the envelope and is somewhat speechless. "I have to get this to the Director; it's above my paygrade" he stammers.

The Attorney General's Office is soon involved, hair on fire. Apparently, there are some political connections. Otto gets his deal and is then put in isolation.

13 Lucinda

It's a week since we busted Otto. Dillion calls Anderson and suggests a meeting with Eyeball's A-Team.

"What do you mean, my A-Team? I only have one team, my All-Stars."

Okay, joking aside, I'd like a meeting tomorrow morning. Can we do that?"

"Does nine work for you?" asks Anderson.

The following morning we are all assembled in the conference/lunchroom when Dillion gets there.

After we get sorted out, everyone with a non-acholic beverage of choice, Dillion starts.

"I've worked with you folks for several years now. I'll be retiring in another year or so, maybe sooner if what I'm going to propose blows up. As you all know we've found one of the backers of the Aryan Brotherhood, the CEO of "Speak-Ezzz." Speak-Ezzz is a relatively new, at least in America, social media platform. The target audience is young adults, and it is growing in popularity. The CEO, Andy Woo, is Chinese and a naturalized US citizen."

"Woo has developed several influential political contacts. The financial trail between him and the Aryan Brotherhood would be enough to indict any run-of-the-mill billionaire. The Attorney General has decided not to indict, claiming the incriminating evidence was improperly obtained. Political pressure is being applied."

"As one of my last acts with the FBI, I want Andy Woo. I'm limited in what I can do within the FBI, so I'm asking if Eyeball would like to take the lead. I'll provide all the support I can."

"That's a mouthful," says Anderson looking around the table.

Without discussion, I say, "I'm in; who's with me?"

Butch and Henry raise their hands. Andy, after some thought, raises his. We look at Anderson.

"What the hell," Anderson says, "let's go for it. I have some contacts in Silicon Valley. What do we know about Woo?"

"Not much," Dillion responds. "He was born in Sichuan Province fifty-three years ago, was sent to the University of Shanghai by China's Peoples Liberation Army. Twenty-five years ago he came to California on a student visa to attend Stanford University. He majored in computer science and was one of their top students."

"He remained in Silicon Valley working under an H1-B visa. Eleven years ago, his application for citizenship was granted. That's when he filed papers for a startup company … Speak-Ezz."

66

"Speak-Ezzz employs several Chinese nationals who are here under the H1 visa program. The company also has close ties with the University of Shanghai, which is a front for the PLA.

"Sounds like a spy organization to me," says Andy.

"It is, and to make matters worse, the company has its tentacles into young adults. Woo curries favor with the 'in crowd' by actively supporting the latest woke nonsense. He's a big contributor to liberal causes. I'm sorry to say he appears to own several Congress members. That's why, I think, the AG is reluctant to indict him."

"Okay, you've made your case Dillion," Anderson says, "what's our game plan?"

"I see a two-prong approach: digital and physical. A strong digital forensics case will take a lot to establish. But to assist in this effort, I have a new FBI analyst willing to work outside the box. If she works on this, she will need facilities here."

"Not a problem," says Anderson. "We have a room in the back of the building she can use."

"Well, to be a bit more specific," Dillion goes on, "she will need at least a half million dollars of state-of-the-art equipment, a dedicated power supply, and an internet trunk line. Oh, and a trailer by the back of the building where she can sleep in her downtime."

We all are staring at Dillion.

"Well don't all speak at once," Dillion says. "To soften the setup expense, I, or rather the FBI can provide a trailer we confiscated from a drug dealer. I also have access to some high-tech equipment that we got from, I'd rather not say where it came from, that Lucinda can pick from as she sets up her lab."

A little dazed, Anderson says she can have as much of the back side of the building that she needs. He notes that there is a backup generator he can upgrade if necessary. As for the internet, Eyeball already has a heavy-duty trunk line. "Let's let Lucinda determine if all this is satisfactory."

The following Monday, an Airstream trailer is delivered. It's placed by the building's back door, and utilities are hooked up. That afternoon small crates from an unknown address start arriving. Early Tuesday, Dillion and Lucinda arrive. Henry is mesmerized. Lucinda is tall, slender, tattooed, and with long red hair. What stands out is her gold nose ring.

"I see the trailer is here," says Dillion. "Have you received any boxes?"

Henry regaining his speech, indicates the back room.

After we regroup in Anderson's office, Dillion introduces us to Lucinda Bjornsson. She's the daughter of Hafþór Júlíus Björnsson, holder of the 'World's Strongest Man' title, and an Italian starlet. "She has her mother's temper and her father's determination," Dillion warns, looking at Henry.

After introductions, Lucinda asks, "Can I see my workspace and get to the packages that have arrived?" without further ado, she grabs Henry and heads to the back of the building.

"Quite an interesting young lady," Anderson muses.

"Don't let appearance deceive you Colonel. Our martial arts instructors won't spar with her; she's deadly. Shortly after we hired her she and I were going to a digital forensics conference in Richmond. We stopped for a travel break at a truck stop. As she was getting coffee, a motorcycle gang came in and their leader started hitting on her. Before I could get to her, she has this behemoth flat on the floor in a fetal position crying for his mommy. That's when she told me she has a black belt in dirty fighting. You might tell Henry to be a gentleman."

"Lucinda," he goes on, "has her doctorate in computer science from Oxford. Last year she snagged a digital forensics certification from MIT. If our project goes sideways, she has a standing offer for a chair at the College of London."

Eyeball's analysts, Caroline and Chloe, are assigned to work with Lucinda. As they get everything unpacked and hooked up, you can hear them muttering under their breaths, "Why can't Anderson get equipment like this for us?"

Before Dillion leaves, Lucinda gives him a list of equipment she still needs. Dillion, in turn, gives it to Anderson. "You can have this stuff tomorrow; it will take me at least a month," and he's gone.

It turns out Lucinda is quite a pleasant person. Eyeball's staff takes to her and helps her to settle in. She tells them, "Once this project is underway, I will be on-site 24/7. I get ideas when I'm relaxing, and I like to pursue them immediately. If I'm hunched over my keyboard, please don't disturb me. Otherwise, please come into my den, and we can chat over a 'cup a.' I snuck an espresso maker into the equipment Dillion sent me."

14 The Hunt

It took Lucinda a little less than a week to infiltrate Speak-Ezzz's internal network. Now the real work began. Sifting through all the files, emails, etc., and culling the material for useful tidbits took time. Announcements for company picnics, employee retirements, new hires, etc., were just shaft. Andy Woo's apparent porn addiction and digital library, well, that was another matter.

It wasn't long before we were sniffing around in Speak-Ezzz's financial records. There were monthly payments going to five members of Congress. There were also small payments, couple thousand bucks each, being made on a routine basis to several accounts around the country.

These small payments piqued my interest. In one of our staff meetings, I brought them up after we discussed payments to the members of Congress. "I see a pattern where there is a series of small payments going to selected States; States who play spoilers in national elections. As we dig deeper into this, recipients of these payments appear to be minor election officials."

"I don't think this is the smoking gun we've been looking for, but what can we do with this information?" comments Anderson

Andy, with a smile, says, "We can mess with their finances. Sean, who was that money launderer you worked with last year, Sydney something? Colonel, can you ask Dillion if we can borrow him for a few days?"

***

The primary season was over. Governor Stillman has a lock on the GOP nomination. all that was left was the convention.

Sarah is back on her protection detail at her request. Just prior to the convention, I was able to pull her away for a weekend getaway, the getaway Dillion disrupted earlier. I was talking with Sarah about the upcoming convention while we were hiking along one of the ridge trails.

"Looks like the Governor has it locked up; what is her campaign team saying?" I ask.

"There are about three States still on the fence. Senator Monroe's home State, but those delegates are wobbly given his poor performance in the primary. Then there are two States that are reluctant to commit to having a black woman as their nominee. You won't read that in the paper, but that is their hang-up. Her team plans to 'out' them early next week as the convention starts. The team expects hundred percent support at the convention. The big question is who her running mate will be."

"What's the feeling about the general election?" I ask.

That's one of their big concerns. It will be close. They think there will be some voter fraud."

"Voter fraud, come now, we've been told that's a myth," I say, tung in cheek.

"How about the opposition? Who are they running?" I continue.

"The Vice President hoped to run, but she can't get any traction. It looks like Pete Mileage, the current Secretary of Transportation, has been tagged. His leadership in the terrorist threat from a couple years ago has thrust him into the limelight."

I met Pete while Eyeball was dismembered the terrorist cells Pete is now taking credit for. I looked at Sarah and said with a smile, "Stillman will have no problem."

***

That Monday when I get back to the Eyeball office, I found Sydney sitting in the lobby.

"Sean, good to see you. Dillion tells me you need my help."

"Let's go into Anderson's office, and he can tell you what we have planned."

Sitting down, coffee in hand, Anderson starts, "Sydney, it's nice to finally meet you. Sean has boasted of your skills. Dillion is impressed with the support you provide the Bureau. Did he tell you about the project we're working on?"

"He told me that if anyone asks I am on vacation. In fact, I'm on a ten-day vacation at a dude ranch in Montana."

Anderson gives Sydney a fairly good rundown of our project, telling him we've identified several payments being made to local election officials. We want those payments redirected to local charities. Payments will probably be recurring up to November. The more interesting money transfers are payments being made to five congressmen. Those payments need to be redirected as anonymous campaign contributions, preferably to those congressman's opponents. It would not hurt if you should 'muddy' some of their campaign funds. Don't take the money but make it unavailable until after the election."

"Colonel, if I may call you that, this should be relatively straightforward," Sydney says.

"Great, one more thing. Dillion lent us a computer genius, Lucinda. She's easily taped into Speak-Ezzz's financial records but doesn't have a financial background. Could you work with her to see what we can do with that information?"

15 Field Work

The general election is just a few weeks away when Anderson calls a meeting. "Our first prong attack on Speak-Ezzz has been a success. We have enough dirt to seriously disrupt Andy Woo's operation. It's time for the second prong so we can kill his operation."

"Sean, I want you, Butch, and Henry, if he's done malingering over that flesh wound, make some field visits. We've identified several election officials who appear to be on the take. Speak-Ezzz money went into their accounts, giving us a money trail, but then was mysteriously donated to local charities," he says with a smile. "I'm sure they are not happy. Your task is to flip these officials and get sworn affidavits. Get some names and follow these names up the feeding chain to Woo."

We decide to work as a team, more intimidating. The nearest election official on our list is in Pennsylvania, Willard Windsor. We corner him in the local coffee shop.

"Willard, we have a problem," I say as I sit down with Butch and Henry taking up positions behind him. "You've been taking money to rig the upcoming election," I say as I lay out some financial statements on the table. "This money can be traced back to a group of foreign agents bent on disrupting the upcoming election."

Willard is getting aggressive, saying, "I don't have any money; it was donated to the Red Cross!"

"I know, we donated it. Now we are not the police, but if these records were turned over to the local officials … well you never know what might happen. And as a bonus, if you don't play ball with us, we'll drain your bank account, your IRA and sell your house. And if you think I'm bluffing, think about how those donations were moved."

Willard slumps in his chair. "What do you want?"

"Names. Who's your handler? Who got you involved in this?"

"He'll kill me."

"As opposed to being charged with aiding a foreign government or, worse yet, a terrorist group. DHS will love getting its hands on you. Give me his name, and he's going down."

"What were you supposed to do?"

Willard takes a deep breath, "I had three tasks," he says.

"Take ballots to retirement homes and get the old biddies to vote the party line. Then deliver the ballots to the polling stations."

"Ballot harvesting, I'm to collect mail-in ballots, weeding out the ones voting for the wrong candidate."

"Finally, when the votes are being counted, do what I can to insert tallies from the cemetery vote."

"You're a busy guy," I say. "We'll meet you here tomorrow at the same time. I will have a lawyer with us and an affidavit detailing this conversation for you to sign. Feel free to bring your own lawyer. If you should be late, we'll donate your house to Habitat for Humanity."

"Have a good day," I say as we walk out of the coffee shop.

Of the twenty-five officials on the list, eighteen cave and sign an affidavit. We will decide what to do with the seven holdouts later.

A single name emerges as the handler. Alex Church. It turns out Alex is in Woo's inner circle. It's a short food chain: election officials, Alex Church, Adam Woo.

In our weekly meeting, I ask Anderson if we should approach Alex now or later.

"Let's let him sit for a while. We don't want the possibility of alerting Woo we're onto him. The bigger question is, who is the link between Speak-Ezzz and the DNC?"

Looking at Lucinda, I ask if she's seen any suggestive email traffic.

"No, but then again, I'm not looking for emails with the subject line Voting Fraud. On a more serious note, I've been looking for a pattern of questionable emails on Speak-Ezzz's server. I can't find any. It's my guess the contact is face-to-face or by snail mail, and only a fool would use snail mail considering the paper trail it leaves."

"You are probably right," says Anderson. "Adam, pull together a small surveillance team to shadow this Church guy. This can be a training exercise for some of our new employees."

"Sean," he continues, "I want you and your team to monitor the more extreme party supporters."

"Gee, thanks," I say, "that's only half the progressive in DC."

"Be creative," he says as the meeting breaks up.

I take my diminished rottweiler team back to my office. "You heard the man; where do we start?"

"I think we should focus on the more radical pundits," Butch says. "They have skin in the game. It would humiliate them if their candidate lost."

"Henry, your thoughts," I ask.

"I was leaning toward academia. On reflection, though, they normally don't have the skill set needed to rig an election. I agree with Butch."

After a little more talk, we narrow the field to a half dozen possible suspects. We take this list to Lucinda and ask if she can scan their digital trails to see what pops up. Two days later, she calls me, a tone of excitement in her voice. "I've found something of interest."

"Mildred Whitehorse, the political opinion editor for the Washington Sun AND who is the niece of Senator Whitehorse, makes periodic trips to Los Vegas."

"So?" I say.

"Alex Church visits Los Vegas on the same dates. It's either a torrid love affair, a coincidence, or we have a smoking gun," says Lucinda.

We up the surveillance on Mildred, Lucinda digging deeper into her digital history, and Butch is dispatched to Washington to monitor her movements.

Within the week, we hit paydirt. Mildred has booked a flight to Las Vegas, and lo and behold, Alex is also headed to Sin City.

As our surveillance teams descend on Los Vegas, Anderson, working with Dillion, has Mildred's reserved room bugged. Alex has no reservations, a little hanky-panky, maybe?

As expected, they both show up in Mildred's room. After some heavy breathing, rustling of bedding, and sighs of contentment Mildred asks, "Everything is set up for the election?"

"Your candidate is going to win by five electoral votes at the minimum. The States we've been working will carry him by at least ten points each. Andy has put fifty million of his own money into this election."

"Fantastic, China will get the trade agreements it wants. Speak-Ezzz will make a fortune, and I get you."

***

By eight-thirty the evening of Election Day, cable commentators are referring to President Stillman. Before the West Coast results are in, she has racked up more than 320 electoral votes.

At eleven that night, Pete Mileage gives his concession speech on CNN. He congratulates Governor Stillman and offers to do what he can to ensure a smooth transition. Meanwhile, progressive pundits are having a meltdown.

Early the following morning the FBI pulls Mildred in, plays a tape for her, and she breaks down, blaming Alex for misleading her. At about the same time, five in the morning, West Coast time, Alex is escorted into the San Francisco regional FBI office. He is indignant, proclaiming his innocence.

The agent states, "We haven't charged you yet; what haven't you done?" As Alex is sputtering a tape is played and a dozen affidavits are laid out in front of him. "You mean election fraud, trying to subvert a presidential election? Boy, your ass is ours!" the agent says.

Alex wants his lawyer. The lawyer is called before the questioning continues. This triggers a call to Andy Woo. Andy grabs a 'go bag' he keeps in his closet and heads to a small airport in Marin County where his Bombardier Global 6000 is kept. He's called ahead; the jet is fueled and on the tarmac, ready to go when he gets there.

The FBI raided Speak-Ezzz's corporate office at ten that morning with a warrant for Woo's arrest. They are told he's on

80

a business trip to Shanghai and is not expected back for some time.

The FBI issued seven arrest warrants for election fraud. Seven local election officials are in for a bad day. There are also five long-serving congressmen who lost their seats to local upstarts. Their campaigns were so lackluster one would think they had no campaign funds.

16 Lakeview

International tempers have cooled. The Mounties are happy, the FBI's happy, and the State Department is happy. I'm happy. President-Elect Stillman is happy. Election officials are trying to hide the mess Woo has left behind.

Sarah and I are on the Eyeball Gulfstream along with Anderson, Butch, and Henry. Henry's side is still tender from, as Anderson likes to call it, 'the bluenose[4] shootout.'

We're headed to Lakeview for a week of partying; it's Mark and Rebecca's Wedding. Henry is the best man, and the rest of us are there for moral support. Mark has faced challenges in the past: drug lords, terrorists, assassins, etc., but he is now facing his biggest challenge, the 'I DO' challenge.

We land at Lakeview's airstrip, and I note there are still no commercial improvements. Mark is there with his SUV, a big dark blue Tahoe, to collect the Eyeball team. Wanda is there to collect Sarah and me. We are staying with Wanda, while the

---

[4] The famous racing ship Bluenose brought its home province of Nova Scotia great pride in the 1920s and 1930s. This nickname is commonly used as an alternative to "Nova Scotian,"

rest of the Eyeball contingent will be housed by the Mayor in his motel, the Best Western Skyline Motor Lodge.

Wanda and the twins, now twelve years old, are thriving. Millie is on the local swim team, and Arnold is planning on trying out for the school's hockey team. Arnold also has a simi-part time job with Jake taking care of Jake's horses.

Wanda's financial adviser business, *Dollars Without Work*, has taken off, leaving her fewer hours than she needs for her family. She is looking to hire, but people with financial planning skills are scarce. She is in discussions with the University of Oregon's graduate program to establish a student training position, a paid position, which would provide hands-on financial planning experience to up-and-coming financial gurus.

Wanda and Sarah hit it off. "It's about time someone took charge of Sean," Wanda is saying, "Anderson keeps sending him on crazy assignments. He's got my kids kidnapped and me held at gunpoint by terrorists. And to him, it's all another day at the office."

Sarah and I are put in the first-floor bedroom suite, which leads to me recounting my time on the run; she's heard it all before, but now sitting on the overstuffed couch, I recounted my story again.

"Sheriff Smith dropped me off here, more years ago than I care to remember, and told me I was an acting doctor. Unbeknownst to me, he and Anderson were in cahoots. After my misunderstanding with the FBI was cleared up, I became his deputy."

As thoughts of Suzie crossed my mind, I changed the topic. "Let's go to Flo's for breakfast in the morning, the best diner in town."

Flo's Diner was open and thriving. Sarah and I walk in, and "well, looky who's back, just like a bad penny," Rossie's voice booms from across the room as she comes to give me a hug. Glancing at Sarah, she continues, "Lady, you can do better than this guy; he can't even keep down a full-time job!"

"And you're looking good to Rossie," I say. "I see you've opened the restaurant area for breakfast. Business must be good." Flo added the restaurant wing to the diner several years ago to accommodate the dinner crowd and larger gatherings. Normally the room was closed for breakfast.

As we are seated, Rossie sliding into the seat on the other side of the booth, says, "Flo passed this last fall. I bought the place, but it will always be Flo's Diner."

"You've been the driving force here for many years; congratulations."

"Oh, but there's more to the story," says Rossie. "When the court was settling her estate, Flo had no will or estate plan, you know. She could have used Wanda's services. The lawyers wanted to close the diner and sell the property to a developer. The Mayor applauded new downtown development … but cautioned potential developers that building permits might be hard to come by given Flo's Diner was a local landmark. The three potential developers read between the lines, and the court sold me the diner as is. Since that fiasco,

I've had to open the restaurant addition for breakfast and hire new staff."

We place our order. I was going to order my usual, but the waitress had no idea what that was. I ended up ordering 'lumberman specials' for Sarah and myself, telling her, "This is the best you'll get anywhere."

As coffee is being served, Mark wanders in looking for me. "I thought I'd find you here."

"You must be Sarah. Rebecca is looking forward to meeting you. I think she wants to compare notes on the rottweilers. Don't overdo the stories; you might scare her off," he says with a grin.

He then turns to me, "Sean, I have an idea that Rebecca and I have been thinking about. Wanda is also a party to this. Rebecca and I have been toying with the idea of leaving the sheriff's department and opening a private investigators' office. We both qualify for Oregon PI Licenses. Wanda tells me she has had a few clients who were looking for an investigator. And as you know, the sheriff's office gets the occasional request for specialized service that they have to turn down. What do you think?"

"Mark, let me think about it for a day or two, and I'll get back to you. But at first glance, your idea might be viable."

Our next stop that morning is the sheriff's office. Walking in, I see one or two old hands that I recognize. "Is the Sheriff in?" I ask the desk sergeant.

"Do you have an appointment?"

"No, but tell the Sheriff Sean is here to reclaim his old job."

The Sargent calls back and before he can put the handpiece back in the cradle, Amanda is rushing toward us. "Sean, you want the job; it's yours. City Hall just cut the department's budget," she says as she gives me a bear hug.

As we are settling into chairs in her office, Amanda offers us coffee. "Thought you'd never ask," I say. "That looks like Smith's old coffee maker. It's probably as old as the building."

I introduce the two ladies; they have a lot in common. Amanda is Lakeview's Sheriff, and Sarah is an FBI agent. They compare notes and exchange a few stories before their conversation turns on me ... at which point I ask Amanda what she thinks of Mark's plan.

Disappointed to be sidetracked, she expresses her concerns about budget cuts and now the possibility of losing her two best deputies.

"Do you want to recommend any of your people to backfill for Mark?" she asks and then continues, "I think it is a good opportunity for the two. There has been a growing need for private investigative services in this part of the State. Conflicts between farmers and ranchers, tourists lost property and an occasional domestic dispute. I also understand Wanda has an occasional case that needs to be unraveled. So yes, I think he and Rebecca can make it work."

We walk back to the car, which is parked in the back of the diner and drive the few blocks to Wanda's office. We find a sleek new building with two floors and an attached reserved

86

parking lot. Entering, we are in a nice lobby looking out to a small courtyard with two office suites, one to the left and one to the right. Stairs and an elevator to the second floor are to the right, where there are two more suites. Wanda's office is to the left on the first floor.

The receptionist is a young lady. I want to say girl; she looks old enough to be a high school student. "Welcome to Dollars Without Work. I don't think I've seen you before. How can we help you?'

"June," the nameplate on the desk identifies her as June Miller, "we're from Florida and need to park a couple million dollars before the drug dealers find us." June's face turns a few shades paler, and she quickly goes into the back office after telling us to have a seat.

I hear Wanda's laugh as she comes through the door. "Dad, why are you scaring June? Good help is hard to find." Wanda turns to June "This is my father; don't believe anything he says. His next story is he's a secret agent looking for terrorists."

June, now much more relaxed, asks if we would like coffee or soda as we go into Wanda's office. "Two coffees," I say and am awestruck by the décor. The office looks like a Wall Street tycoon's inner sanctum.

Wanda is watching me and says, "Decoration is in memory of Jeffrey. His investments are making this all possible."

Jeffrey was Wanda's deceased husband. Turns out he was the East Coast mob's money launderer. After helping the

FBI bring down the mob, he was gunned down in the street. During the FBI operation, Wanda and the kids were placed in a Lakeview safe house. She decided to stay. Jeffrey's investments were a bit north of seventeen million. But to be fair to Jeffery, the money Wanda inherited as co-owner of the Swiss account was based on Jeffery's shrewd investments, not mob money.

With coffee in hand, I tackle the question that brought me here. "Mark was telling me he and Rebecca are considering going into the private detective business. He seems to think you can throw some business his way. Do they have a viable plan?"

"I think so," says Wanda. "I get six or eight customers a year who ask for references for a good investigator. Various reasons given, but they feel they need those services. I've also talked with Amanda, and she receives requests for specialized services the sheriff's office can't provide. I've told Mark he can have the vacant office upstairs; you know I own this building, rent-free until he has an established business. So, to answer your question, Mark and Rebecca are sitting on a gold mine."

17 Nuptials

The day has arrived. It's mid-November, and whereas past years have seen a foot of snow on the ground by now, it's a mild fall with daytime temperatures in the mid-50s.

Rossie is hosting breakfast for all the wedding attendees. There is the Eyeball contingent, the Sheriff's office, several town officials, and members of Rebecca's extended family.

Rebecca McKay is a local girl, a graduate of a local college and not wanting to go into the family business, majored in criminal justice. The family business, half the cattle ranches in central Oregon. In the early 1840's her people followed the Oregon Trail and staked out a huge tract of land. Her g-g-grandfather William McKay opened a trading post in what later became Pendleton, Oregon. The town was named after another of her relatives, George Pendleton, a 19th-century politician and diplomat.

Rossie was beside herself, trying to find seats for everyone. I stepped into the breach and taped my water glass with my fork getting the crowd's attention.

"Folks, we have an overflow crowd this morning who have come to wish the bride and groom the best," I said as I tilted my head to the two who were sitting in the corner booth. "The ceremony will be at noon today at the Methodist Church on 8th Street. Perhaps those of you who have finished might like to freshen up before the ceremony and relinquish your seat to those who are running late."

My audience turned and resumed their conversations, but given a few minutes, several tables started to empty with departing customers waving to the bride and groom.

As Rossie approached me "Sean, thanks; breakfast is on the house for the rest of your visit."

As I was sitting down, Wanda was saying to the table, "I think Sean just evicted us. You are all invited to come up to my home for refuge, and I think I can find some coffee and danish." The folks from the two tables we were occupying moved out to the parking lot, and a small cavalcade headed up into the foothills.

Pulling into the circular drive, Anderson said, "This is the hovel Smith put you in? It's the best log cabin I've ever seen."

"I spent six months here, Colonel, and I never saw it all. I was afraid to leave the bedroom at night for fear of getting lost."

We all enter the great room and I'm thinking to myself, this is the first time I've seen this room full of people, and noted there was still room to move. Anderson and I gravitate to overstuffed chairs by the fireplace.

"Colonel, you and the Eyeball's crew being here means a lot to Mark." We chat for a while before I tell him of Mark's plans. He nods and moves on to a new topic.

"Sean, did I tell you the Canadian Coast Guard was impressed with your speedy departure this spring? As a peace offering, I introduced their Commandant to Philip Boswell. Boswell Maritime Repairs is now under contract to provide them with three boats. I suggest one should be christened Sean's Escape."

As he continues reflecting on the summer's activities, he mentions Sydney, that he would hire him if he didn't have a court-driven commitment to the FBI. "He's an amazing guy. He and Lucinda were able to track Woo's money to senior members in the administration, including two accounts in the Cayman Islands. We turned the information over to Dillion. Dillion is threatening to go public if the Attorney General doesn't follow up. I've also put a bug in President-Elect Stillman's ear. All-in-all, it's been a good year."

***

Time moves on, and it was soon time to go to the church … which was packed. The only way Sarah and I got a seat was one pew was reserved for the groom's family: Sarah, Wanda, myself, and the Eyeball contingent. Rebecca recruited the twins to be part of the wedding party; Millie was the flower girl, and Arnold was the ring bearer.

The wedding went off without a hitch; it could have been the centerpiece for a bride's magazine.

Rossie was a bit miffed that she wasn't asked to cater the reception, but was thankful she hadn't been after seeing the crowd. Rebecca's parents had rented a field on the edge of town not far from the Lakeview airstrip. They erected a circus size tent and flew in a prestigious catering service from Portland. Rossie was captivated by the portable kitchen that had been set up. The tent was filled with Rebecca's extended family and a few politicians. This was the biggest shindig Lakeview ever saw.

Later that afternoon, the Colonel cornered Mark and, with the Eyeball people, thanked him for his time with the company. He expressed regret for the scratches he received in Mexico taking down El Honcho, downplaying how close to death Mark was when he arrived on the emergency helipad.

"Mark, I understand you and Rebecca are planning on becoming private investigators. My hat is off to you; it's a challenge for anyone who ventures into the private sector with a new enterprise. As I told you when you first jumped ship to become a deputy sheriff, I have your back. Let me double down on that. If in your investigations, you need a deep dive into someone's background, Eyeball's analysts are available to you. Please call if we can be of help. And who knows, I might be a future customer.

END